PANDA books are for young readers
making their own way
through books.

O'BRIEN SERIES FOR YOUNG READERS

O'BRIEN panda cubs

O'BRIEN pandas

O'BRIEN panda legends

 O'BRIEN flyers

Snobby Cat

PATRICK DEELEY

• Pictures by Tatyana Feeney •

THE O'BRIEN PRESS
DUBLIN

First published 2005 by The O'Brien Press Ltd,
12 Terenure Road East, Rathgar, Dublin 6, Ireland.
Tel: +353 1 4923333; Fax: +353 1 4922777
E-mail: books@obrien.ie
Website: www.obrien.ie
Reprinted 2006, 2011.

ISBN: 978-0-86278-946-6

British Library Cataloguing-in-Publication Data
Deeley, Patrick, 1953-
Snobby cat
1.Snobs and snobbishness - Juvenile fiction 2.Cats - Juvenile fiction
3.Children's stories
I.Title II.Feeney, Tatyana
823.9'14[J]

The O'Brien Press receives assistance from

3 4 5 6 7 8 9 10
11 12 13 14

Typesetting, layout, editing, design: The O'Brien Press Ltd
Printing: Cox & Wyman Ltd
The paper in this book is produced using pulp from managed forests.

Can YOU spot the panda
hidden in the story?

Orlando wasn't just
any old cat.
He was a
Persian Black Smoke –
with long flowing fur
and large, amber eyes.

What's more, he lived
in the biggest, grandest house
in the village.

Each morning,
Orlando
would stand on a
pedestal
while his owner,
Bertha Browne,
groomed
his fur.

Not a single
hair could be
left out
of place.

Orlando didn't take milk.
Oh no! He drank cream
from a china bowl.

And he slept
in a basket
filled with silk cushions.

But one night
when Orlando couldn't sleep,
he slipped through the cat-flap
out to the garden.

The moon shone,
bringing a gleam to his eye.
Orlando made gentle
twirls and twists
on the garden path.

'O my!' he said. 'I've never
had such wild fun!'

Suddenly he stopped.

What were those
shadowy shapes
slinking slowly
through the flowerbeds?

Yes! It was those beastly cats
from Caterwaul Corner.
What were they doing
in **his** garden?

One fellow was
missing an eye.
A second had only half an ear.
A third hopped on three legs.
A fourth had lost his tail.

The Caterwaul Corner cats
jumped on each other,
making a mad, furry ball.

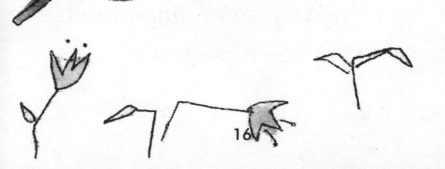

'How common,' Orlando hissed.
'Clear off, you mangy cats!'

The cats stopped
just long enough to snigger
at Orlando.
Then they turned back
to wrestle and roll
among the flowerbeds again.
'I must let Bertha know,'
Orlando cried.

He saw a large flowerpot
on the window-sill.
He leaped up, and the pot fell
with a loud crash.

The window of Bertha's room
shot open.
'Away, you scruffy cats!'
she shrieked.

A vaseful of water
came tumbling down –
right on top of Orlando,
drenching him to the bone.

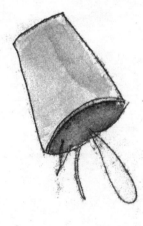

The tomcats fled.
Orlando just stood
and shivered.

Next morning Orlando's fur
was still wet.

It stood all on end,
making him look
spiky as a hedgehog.

He had to stand on his pedestal
for two whole hours
while Bertha sprayed
and shampooed
and groomed him.

fancy cat
shampoo

Only when he
was looking his best
could he come to sit at table.

There was cream,
and there was cheese
on a board.
There was butter in a dish.
And there was salmon!

'Breakfast, my darling!'
said Bertha.

Orlando smiled.
Everything was back to normal.

After dinner,
he crept onto Bertha's
lap as she was
sleeping beside
the sitting-room
fire. He began
to doze.

Tap-tip.

Scritch.

Scrip-scrap!

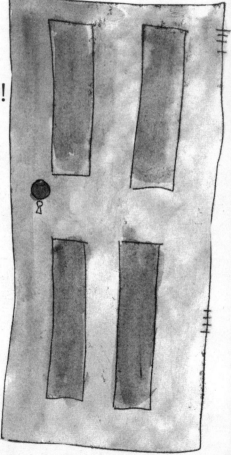

What was that?
Noises coming from
the spare room?

Orlando opened one eye,
and twitched one ear.

Suddenly Orlando was flung
into the air.
Bertha had woken up.

'**Mice**! **Mice**!' she screamed.

'Orlando, go up and catch
those dreadful creatures
at once,' she ordered.

Orlando stared at Bertha
from the fireside rug,
where he had landed.

Me? he thought.
How can she ask **me**
to catch **mice**?

But he knew those mice
would have to be caught.
And it would be **his** job.

Slowly he climbed the stairs.
He pushed open
the spare-room door.

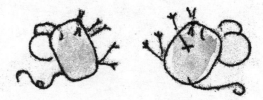

'Yuck!' he said.
He could smell the mice.
'I'm afraid of mice!'

Orlando turned and ran.
He ran into Bertha's bedroom,
jumped over Bertha's bed
and out through
the open window.

He tumbled down
to the garden below,
and landed
almost on his feet.

'I know what I'll do,'
he gasped.
'I'll hire a **mouse-hunter**.'

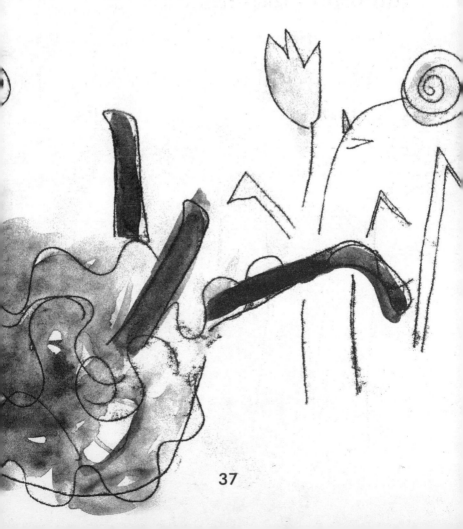

He saw a magpie perched
on a chimney pot.
'I'm a nest-robber,
not a mouse-hunter,'
the magpie sneered.
'Find a hawk
if you're too lazy
to catch the mice yourself.'

Orlando had no idea
where to look for a hawk.
He went to the park.

Above his head
he saw a kite
and the smoky trail of a jet,
but no hawk.

Orlando stroked his whiskers
and thought and thought.
'The alley cats!' he said at last.
'I'll get **them** to help.'

He strolled to Caterwaul Corner
and looked around.
'Where can they be?'
he wondered.

Suddenly a bin lid
fell with a clatter.

A man-hole cover lifted.

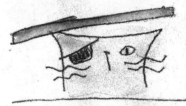

An old door creaked open.

One by one,
the Caterwaul cats came out.
They smirked
and winked slyly.

They stood in a circle
around Orlando.

'I was wondering,'
Orlando said,
clearing his throat,
'if you guys would catch
some mice for me
up at Bertha's house?'

The Caterwaul cats blinked
and scratched themselves
with their long, dirty nails.

'Why don't you catch them
yourself?' One-Eye hissed.

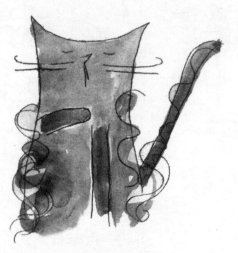

'Well,' said Orlando,
'only common cats catch mice.
And, you see,
I am **not** a common cat.'

'Too posh to catch mice!'
Three-Legs sniggered.
'Tell us, what kind of cat
is a cat who won't catch mice?'

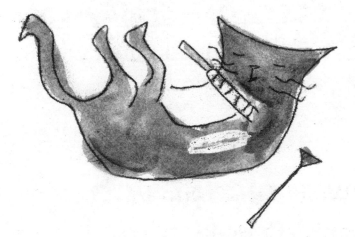

'He's no cat,' Half-Ear snarled.
'He's a chicken!'

'Maybe he's a **mouse**!'
laughed No-Tail.

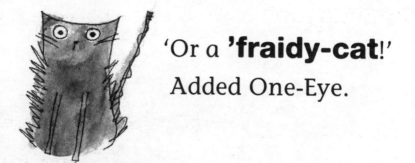

'Or a **'fraidy-cat**!'
Added One-Eye.

'He's a **catastrophe**!
yelled Three-Legs.
They all rolled around,
laughing.

Then the Caterwaul Corner cats
rushed at Orlando,
hissing and spitting.

Orlando ran.

What will I do? he wondered.
I can't go home now.
I must get those mice.

Night came.
Orlando crept back to
Bertha's garden.
He climbed into the branches
of an oak tree and gazed sadly
in at his old home.

Next moment he heard
a ghostly voice.
'**Hooo**! **Hooo**!
I can get rid of the mice.'

Orlando jumped.
He nearly fell out of the tree.
He was staring
into the large, round eyes
of a barn owl.

'There's a hole under the roof,'
she whispered.
'I can go through it
and eat up all the mice.'

'But why?'
asked Orlando.
'Why do **you**
want to help me?'

'I don't,' said the owl.
'But mice are my
favourite food!
And I'd like the spare room
to myself every day
so I can sleep in peace.'

'It's a deal,'
said Orlando.
'Don't let Bertha
find out!'

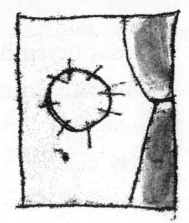

Next morning Bertha
listened for the mice.

Nothing! Not a **scritch!**

Not a **scratch!**

'They're gone!' she said.
She gathered Orlando
up in her arms.
'**My hero**!'
she beamed.
Orlando was
delighted.

No 1
mouse
catcher

Orlando's problem was solved.

But there was a catch.

One day the owl
wanted Orlando's **cream**.

Then she wanted his **salmon**!

And his silk
cushions!

Poor Orlando!
Now he was a servant
to a **bird**!

Where would it all end?